Sheep Don't Count Sheep

MARGARET WISE BROWN

illustrated by BENREI HUANG

Margaret K. McElderry Books
New York   London   Toronto   Sydney   Singapore

Sleep, little lamb, and dream your dream
of things that are as things would seem.
Dream of a world you want to keep,
of soft green grasses long and deep.
Deep and warm and safe in sleep,
little lamb, now go to sleep.

A little sheep was going to sleep;
a little soft white lamb of a sheep,
quietly, softly was going to sleep.

But every time his soft head nodded
and his eyes blinked closed, he saw
something else happening around him.

A bug jumped off a grass blade.

A horse jumped up in the air.

An ant pinched a grasshopper and made it hop.

"How can I sleep?" said the sleepy little sheep to his mother, who stood over him. "Every time I start to go to sleep, I see something happen."

"Close your eyes," baaaaaaed the mother
sheep, "and count butterflies.

"Count butterflies fluttering past your
closed eyes till you fall asleep, . . .

". . . little sleepy sheep."

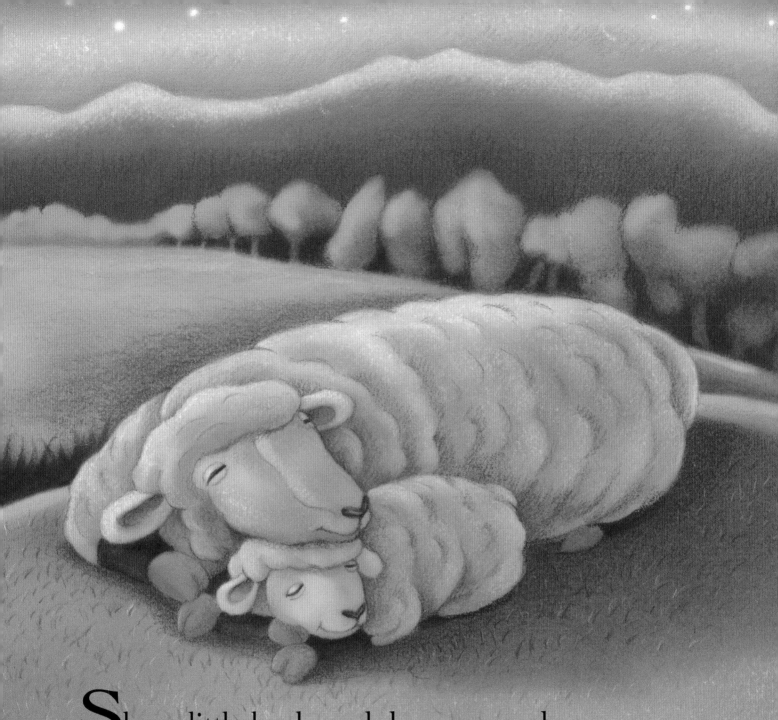

Sleep, little lamb, and dream your dream
of things that are as things would seem.
Dream of a world you want to keep,
of soft green grasses long and deep.
Deep and warm and safe in sleep,
little lamb, now go to sleep.

Sleep, Little Lamb

Music by Emily Gary McCormick and Annette Carpenter-Wawerna

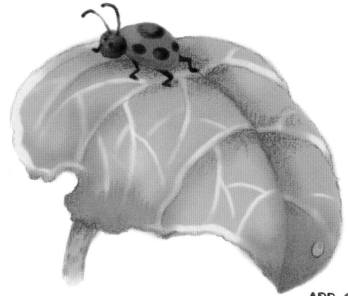

APR 1 5 2003

For a very special couple,
Judith and Marty,
who count bugs with my son
—B. H.

Margaret K. McElderry Books
An imprint of Simon & Schuster Children's Publishing Division
1230 Avenue of the Americas
New York, NY 10020

Book design by Abelardo Martínez
The text of this book is set in Cochin.
The illustrations are rendered in watercolor and color pencils.
Printed in Hong Kong
2 4 6 8 10 9 7 5 3 1
Library of Congress Cataloging-in-Publication Data
Brown, Margaret Wise, 1910–1952.
Sheep don't count sheep / by Margaret Wise Brown ; illustrated by Benrei Huang.— 1st ed.
p. cm.
Summary: A little lamb has trouble falling asleep, until his mother
tells him to count the butterflies that flutter past his closed eyes.
ISBN 0-689-83346-6
[1. Sheep—Fiction. 2. Sleep—Fiction.] I. Huang, Benrei, ill. II. Title.
PZ7.B8163 Sgp 2002
[E]—dc21
00-046070

FIRST EDITION